# Disney
# PIRATES of the CARIBBEAN
# JACK SPARROW

## Bold New Horizons

by Rob Kidd

Illustrated by Jean-Paul Orpinas

Based on the earlier life of the character, Jack Sparrow,
created for the theatrical motion picture,
"Pirates of the Caribbean: The Curse of the Black Pearl"
Screen Story by Ted Elliott & Terry Rossio and Stuart Beattie and Jay Wolpert,
Screenplay by Ted Elliott & Terry Rossio,
and characters created for the theatrical motion pictures
"Pirates of the Caribbean: Dead Man's Chest" and
"Pirates of the Caribbean: At World's End"
written by Ted Elliott & Terry Rossio

Disney PRESS

New York

Special thanks to
Liz Braswell, Rich Thomas, and Ken Becker

To my wife, Joslyn Siminski, for all her love and support.
Love you babe.
—Jean-Paul

# Bold New Horizons

~~Dear Diary,~~

~~My Executive Journal~~

Captain's Log

Well, it's been a while since I've written in you, mate. Of course, life has been pretty exciting for the last year—far too much going on to be able to spend any time sitting at a desk and jotting down thoughts.

Why, just now I've come out the other side of an engagement with Captain Torrents _and_ the leaders of the Scaly Tails _and_ thousands and thousands of their nasty Scaly-Tailed legions. It was a terrible time, but you can be sure that yours truly, Captain Jack Sparrow, carried himself with bravery and valiance.

Indeed, if it weren't for my cleverness, my daring, all the buckles that I swashed and all the merfolk I personally dispatched, well, things would be a lot darker now, I can tell you. It might be said—no, it _should_ be said—that I, Captain Jack Sparrow, single-handedly saved the Seven Seas. You can all sail free and clear, safe from Torrents and his Scaly-Tail army, thanks to my derring-do.

In fact, that's about all I've been doing for the past year! Saving people here, making the world safe there—rescuing my crew from first one danger, then another. No time for myself at all, really.

Just around a year ago—let's say a year ago this coming Monday, just to give this all an air of legitimacy—I ran away from home I liberated myself from the stranglehold of my family's influence. I was sick to death of Da and second-auntie "Quick Draw" McFleming and Grandmama with all her blasted blades and "pirates" this and "pirates" that.

So I stowed away and betook myself to Tortuga, where some noisome pirate stole the bag containing my only worldly possessions. I tried to steal it back. Only, I stole the _wrong_ bag, from a very _wrong_ pirate—the cursed Captain Torrents. The bag didn't contain my things, but instead the scabbard of the legendary Sword of Cortés, a toothsome treasure if there ever was one.

(None of this would have happened, by the way, if it hadn't been for Captain Smith and—oh, never mind. More on that later . . .)

In Tortuga, I met Arabella, whom I refer to as Bell, mostly because it annoys her.

Bell recognized my obvious and innate captaincy and pledged her loyalty immediately. The eventually diabolical Fitzwilliam P. Dalton the Third, whom I refer to as Fitzy, mostly because he annoys me, also leaped at the chance to join my crew, and we acquired the mighty ship

_Barnacle_ and sailed away to great adventure, looking for the Sword of Cortés. Along the way we visited desert island number one and picked up a mangy cat and her two keepers, the Mayan sailor Tumen and his Creole companion, Jean.

Long story short, Torrents apparently wanted the sheath to the Sword of Cortés back. It held great power, and it was also key in the mission he'd been sent on by the feared captain of the ghost ship _Flying Dutchman_, Davy Jones. Said feared captain had actually cursed Torrents with the ability to conjure storms when he's angry. Useful, but uncontrollable.

I brilliantly defeated Torrents, of course. We were still looking for the Sword when my crew was ensnared by the quite annoying and off-key song of the blasted Scaly Tails (or mermaids as you might call them). I call them Scaly Tails mostly because they annoy me and I like to annoy them right back. After having to run around keeping my crew safe from themselves (it's a long story, but I hear they've written a book about it called The Siren Song, if you're interested in hearing it all), I cleverly bargained with the Scaly Tails for the crew's release. And so we arrived on deserted island number two, where I had to battle another notorious pirate, Left-Foot Louis and his deadly army of murderous pirates. Not surprisingly—well, at least, not surprisingly to me—I managed, through

more of the aforementioned trickery and bravery,
finally to acquire the Sword of Cortés . . .

. . . Which resurrected the Sword's original,
most vicious (and probably stinkiest) owner,
Hernán Cortés. Is all this too hard for you
to swallow, dear ~~diary~~ ~~journal~~ Captain's Log?
Well, then, batten down ye hatches. . . . It gets
even better.

In order to defeat him, I needed to revisit
the Scaly Tails—which was not fun—in order to
acquire the one charmed object that could overcome
an undead lunatic like Herny. (I call him
Herny because I think it's much funnier than
Hernán.)

Shortly after, I needed to save my crew from

7

freezing. In a snowstorm. On a deserted island. In the Caribbean. It's like they go <u>looking</u> for trouble that lot.

So now, free of swords and gods and curses and snow, we set sail, intending to drop Jumen and Jean and their stupid cat, Constance, off in some backwater village in the Yucatán, when I got wind of the lovely and powerful Sun-and-Stars amulet that could turn things into gold and make me the richest, and therefore most powerful, and therefore freest, sailor in the world.

I don't know what the most tiresome part of that journey was—saving New Orleans from being turned into metal, destroying the many-headed serpent pirate—well, she wasn't really a pirate per se; let's say pirateish—queen—Madame Minuit, or meeting Bell's mum, an annoying pirate captain with a ship called the Fleur de la Mort what can turn itself invisible, who took my crew along with her. Took 'em all.

. . . With the exception of ye ole Fitzy. That left just Fitzy and me and his ridiculous priyed possession—a little pocket watch which he never went anywhere without. Then suddenly, Davy Jones wanted the watch. That was when I began to think . . . hmmm . . . perchance the pocket watch was not so ridiculous after all.

Apparently, the foppish boy's watch had some ability to control time, or destroy it altogether, or some nonsense like that. Luckily, I was around

to save the Caribbean—if not the world—
again.

   And what do I ever get for all this
world-saving, mind you? Not even a pat on the
back. Not even a simple "Cheers, mate. Thank
you, Captain Jack Sparrow."

   Only thing I ever get is trouble. And the
next time it showed up, it was in the form of the
dread pirate Teague, Keeper of the Pirate
Code. Oh, some say Teague is my dad, by the
way.

   I learned Fitzy was a spy working for the
navy, using me to look for Teague. So, of course,
it was up to me to rescue Dad and battle the
Royal Navy. All by myself, mind you.

Then the Royal Navy blew up the _Barnacle_. You would think that that would be just about the proper amount of action, adventure, pirate problems, swashbuckling, and scallywaging a poor old mate would be allotted for his lifetime. No such luck.

As I sailed off into the sunset on the dingy little boat I rented, I found another bloody stray to look after. A certain pirate by the name of Billy Turner. Bloody Billy, as I called him (oh, come on, it's not that mean; he was chopped up like raw hamburger when I found him), had me running from a pirate crew that he said was after the very same treasure I was looking for—the fabled Trident of Poseidon.

11

Of course, as might have been be expected from the path of my life and the twists and turns it takes, the other pirates turned out to be my old crew—Arabella, Jumen, Jean, Constance (ugh), and Bell's mum, Captain Smith (ugh, ugh), and her first mate, Mr. Reece.

We learned that the Trident was in the possession of the feared Captain Torrents (see the beginning of this entry if the length of my story has caused you to forget that he was my first adversary in this whole mess of an adventure). Of course, dangerous cursed pirate plus powerful trident plus mermaids equals disaster.

So the Blue-tailed mermaids—there seem to

be only three and they appear to rule over all the others; their names are Morveren, Aquila, and Aquala—begged me to help them get the Trident back. Apparently it was actually _theirs_, and had been for hundreds of years. Powerful stuff, that Trident. It can summon earthquakes and tsunamis and, most interestingly, control the entire population of merfolk. Cept for the aforementioned blue Scaly Tails.

Which of course left me, Jack Sparrow, to save my old, traitorous crew, and the world, from stinky merfolk-and-Torrents domination. What else is new? I ask you.

But that's a tale too terrible and wondrous for me to tell. (Plus, I wouldn't want to be doing all of the bragging about how brave and daring I was.

So I guess you will have to wait until someone writes a book about how I defeated Torrents for the last time.

Ta-ta for now.

Signed,
~~Jack Sparrow~~
Captain Jack Sparrow

# CHAPTER ONE

Captain Torrents gripped Poseidon's Trident. A storm cloud brewed around his head. He laughed and howled like a madman.

He stood in the ruins of a cavern deep beneath Poseidon's Peak, a mountain beneath the sea. His filthy hair was wet and matted and clung to his head like a net of wiry filth. His clothes were torn: a pant leg was missing, and his shirt was in tatters, rags blowing around his arms and chest. His complexion was pale, broken up by even paler scars that crisscrossed his skin. His eyes sparked like lightning, and he grinned with a skeleton's smile of broken and rotten teeth.

"You might want to have a sawbones take a look at that, mate. Or get yerself acquainted with a toothbrush," Jack Sparrow said.

"*Jack!*" everyone else in the cavern scolded.

"Everyone else" was a who's who of all the people who had been important in Jack's life over the past year. Captain Laura Smith stood bravely, still somehow proud and immaculate while up to her boots in debris and seawater that spilled in through the shattered cave walls. Standing close by was the dashingly handsome Mr. Reece, Laura's first mate aboard her ship, the *Fleur de la Mort*. Jean and Tumen, the plucky Creole and Mayan sailors who just wanted to end their adventures and spend the rest of their lives on a beach, stood close by. Constance, the mangy cat who was supposedly Jean's sister under a curse, was snug in her brother's arms. While she *could* swim, she preferred not to.

Arabella, Jack's old first mate, aboard his previous ship, the *Barnacle*—and one of the *best* first mates a captain could have—was there, gripping the arm of the tortured-soul-turned-reluctant-pirate Billy Turner.

In the marble-rimmed pool that commanded the center of the room were the three leaders of the merfolk: Morveren, Aquila, and Aquala. Their blue tails thrashed in the water.

"You will all pay!" Torrents screamed. Droplets of foamy spittle fell to the ocean.

"Ugh," Jack said, taking a step back. Even the usually ice-cold Laura Smith looked a little uncertain. She shifted in her boots.

Then she set her jaw and strode forward, a scowl on her face, a true pirate queen. Jack couldn't help being a little impressed.

"Do you have something to say for yourself, then, Smith?" Torrents demanded.

"That's *Captain* Smith, you shipless mutt," she shot back. "I should have killed you properly back in Tortuga."

"Oh, you were quite the captain back then," Torrents said, rolling his eyes. "Speaking of shipless."

"Wait, these two know each other?" Jean asked, confused.

"Pirating's a pretty small circle these days," Jack said airily, as if he knew. Which, in fact, he sort of did. It was his family's trade, after all.

"*Ach*, and what were you?" Captain Smith asked Torrents. She rolled her eyes and turned to face the crew. "You lot should have seen him. Before he was cursed by Davy Jones. Before he had power over the seas and waters. Before he had the Trident. Just another scrawny seadog. I think he and his crew were captured more times than he actually set sail."

"Smith . . ." Torrents growled warningly.

"Oh, I'm not making it up, am I?" she whirled on him. "Your biggest haul was a boatload of bananas on its way from Jamaica!"

"Mum . . ." Arabella said pleadingly, worried by the look on Torrents's face.

"And do ye know what the name of his mighty ship was?" Captain Smith leaned forward as if imparting a great secret.

"It were a fine ship . . ." Torrents said, a little sadly.

"*The Monkeebutt!*" Captain Smith announced with great smugness.

Jack smirked. Jean and Tumen could barely contain themselves. Even the usually stoic Billy Turner smiled.

The mermaid queen, Morveren, just raised an eyebrow.

Torrents slammed his trident down on the ground, causing the cavern to quake.

"Silence! Perhaps it was that I was 'so easily taken' by the navy because a *certain someone* tipped them off to where my next attack might be!" Torrents continued, pointing his finger accusingly at Arabella's mother.

Everyone looked at Captain Smith in shock.

She tried to affect a look of surprised nonchalance.

It didn't work.

Finally she gave up, and let go an exasperated sigh. "I'm a pirate. That's what we do. What do you want from me?"

"Oh, aye," Torrents growled. "And as it says in the Pirate Code, under the subsection 'Revenge,' I followed you to Tortuga to murder your sorry, betraying hide!"

"It's only betrayal if I claimed to be loyal to you," Captain Smith pointed out reasonably. "I *never* liked you."

"Um, excuse me, mate," Jack said, putting up a hand like a schoolboy. Something had occurred to him. "Did you say *Tortuga*? When, uh, approximately, was that? Just, you know, for accuracy's sake."

"It was a big, full moon, round and shiny as a gold doubloon," Torrents said, surprisingly poetic. "Last fall."

Jack did a quick mental calculation. Last fall he had been a stowaway. A wet and cold one, who entered a certain bar on Tortuga and met a certain barkeep who became his first mate, the same night that he accidentally stole a certain sack from a certain pirate, thinking it was his own.

"Oh, yes. Revenge, right. I remember now," Captain Smith said, laughing. "You couldn't even do that right. You were all revenge this and get-her-at-sword-point that, and then some little brat goes and steals your luggage, and suddenly revenge is the last thing on your mind. . . ."

"Hey!" Jack said, offended, as *he* was the brat Laura was speaking about.

"Wait," Arabella piped up. "You were on Tortuga? Why didn't you come see me? I thought you were dead!"*

"Hold on just a moment," Jack said, interrupting. "If this conversation goes

*Up until Captain Smith reemerged in Arabella's life, Arabella believed her mother to be dead. She recounts this horrible story in Vol. 3, *The Pirate Chase.*

off its tracks it should be me who derails it. Let me get this straight: if you, Captain Laura Smith, hadn't repeatedly turned you, Captain Torn-Pants, over to the Royal Navy, *you* Captain Torn-Pants wouldn't have sworn revenge on her, Laura Smith, which means you wouldn't have come to Tortuga, which means you wouldn't have followed . . . which means *I* wouldn't have accidentally stolen your . . ." Jack waved his hand looking for the right word. ". . . Luggage."

Torrents and Captain Smith both looked at him, shrugging and nodding.

"Aye, so?" Torrents asked.

"So?" Jack cried. "All this folderol I've been through in the last year . . . cursed swords, being chased by the navy, going backward and forward in time with that stupid watch, dealing with the blasted Scaly

Tails . . . All of that could have been avoided had *you*"—he pointed at Captain Smith— "simply not ticked off Captain Torrents here, sending him to Tortuga after you, setting in motion all of the aforesaid adventures?"

Everyone—Arabella, Billy, Jean, Tumen, the three merfolk, and even Constance— looked at Jack in confusion.

"Oh, never mind," Jack sighed, giving up. He waved at Torrents and Smith. "As you were. Carry on with your little back-and-forth." He stepped back with a bow.

"Well, as long as you're talking about revenge and the Code," Captain Smith said, taking up their fight again, "you must know that there is a very specific passage in the Code that mentions the Trident! No pirate shall have his own possession of the mythic weapon! It's too powerful and too dangerous."

"Well, who needs the Code anymore

when you have a weapon this powerful?" Torrents asked.

"You see? This is exactly what I'm talking about," Captain Smith said in exasperation. "Only further evidence of your not being worthy enough for the title *pirate*. Captured by the navy, ignoring the Code . . ."

"'Worthy?'" Tumen asked with mild amusement. "*Pirate* is a title?"

"It is very important to them, like secret handshakes and the Brotherhood," Jean said, shrugging.

"It's a way of life, dear boys," Captain Smith interjected, placing a hand on Tumen's shoulder. "One that our friend Torrents here could not keep up with."

Torrents roared with anger, and struck the ground with the Trident. The entire cavern shook again. Pulverized rock began to crumble, and more fissures appeared in the walls, growing like scary black vines.

And then the water began to rush in.

Jack's eyes widened as a hole opened up near him. He quickly stuck a his hand in to seal it.

And then another hole opened.

Jack stuck his other hand in.

And then another, and another.

He was trying to figure out how to stuff his boot in when he finally gave up: the walls were cracking open, and the sea was pouring in everywhere.

"You and your crew . . ." Torrents began. "*Crews*," he said, correcting himself, looking at Jack, "have interfered with me for the last time."

"Ummm," Jean said, nervously. "My friend and I here are part of no one's crew. We are retired."

"And you'd best not have been implying,

Torrents, that I am aligned with any crew but my own," Captain Smith interjected.

"Uh, excuse me yet again," Jack said, taking his right hand out of the hole in the cavern wall to hold it up like a schoolboy yet again. A stream of water shot over his shoulder. "In case ye hadn't noticed, there's a flood of water pouring in, and as there's no place really for us to run, there's a surprisingly good likelihood that we *are* all going to drown, whoever is crew and who is not."

The cavern shuddered again as seawater weakened the walls. Another portion of the ceiling gave way. Constance meowed. Billy pulled Arabella tightly to him. Captain Smith looked mildly concerned. Tumen and Mr. Reece began banging the walls with the pommels of their weapons, trying to find secret escape routes that didn't involve holding their breath underwater forever.

"Admittedly, I could, with just one more blow, cause the entire cavern to collapse down on ye," Torrents said thoughtfully. "But I've decided to bless ye with a little extra time . . . time in which ye can do nothing but watch the water grow higher and higher until ye drown!"

He slammed the Trident against a wall. Sparks flew.

Coursing through one of the larger holes in the wall came two magnificent blue horses—the ones Jack and Billy had recently freed from being buried on the island.*

They were *Poseidon's* horses, and they pulled the god's ornately carved coral chariot. They danced lightly in place, treading the top of the rising water with pearly hooves.

"Farewell, ye doomed!" Torrents called as

*In Vol. ii, *Poseidon's Peak.*

he leapt up into the chariot and grabbed the reins. He flicked them viciously, and the horses took off down one of the tunnels, churning the water into foam as they went.

The crew watched them go. The merfolk appeared unaffected by these most recent events. After all, they could breathe underwater.

"I'd say we have about a quarter hour before the water reaches the ceiling," Mr. Reece said, raising an eyebrow and gauging the speed of the water, which was now up to the crew's knees.

"Thank you," Jack said through gritted teeth. "That helps ever so much."

# CHAPTER TWO

"And thank *you* for starting all this," Jack added in a huff, turning to Captain Smith. "If old Captain Torn-Pants hadn't come after you, none of us would be here. Now. Wet. About to drown."

"While I'm still not sure I follow you," Captain Smith replied icily, "it is entirely your own fault if you got involved in the little tête-à-tête between myself and Torrents."

"Or grabbed the wrong bag from the

wrong man, ye dolt," Arabella added, reminding Jack that what had really made Torrents Jack's enemy was the fact that Jack had stolen the pirate's bag.

"Um . . . accident," Jack said.

"Yer accident, yer responsibility, Jack!" Arabella retorted.

"Since when do you take your mum's side in these arguments?" Jack asked.

"I just think ye have to start takin' some responsibility fer yerself, Jack!"

"That's all very well and good," Billy Turner sad sadly, pulling Arabella even closer to him, "but what matters all that now? We are all doomed to death by drowning. Only the gods know how far under the sea this cavern really is."

"Oh, you've got yourself a great one, there, Bell," Jack said, taunting Arabella and her new beau, Billy. "Real positive, upbeat, thinking nothing but happy-go-lucky thoughts."

"He is a little morbid, doll," Mr. Reece agreed.

Arabella shot him a look that unmistakably read: *Don't you dare call me doll.*

Jack turned his attention to the merfolk.

"You Scaly Tails must know a way out. You've been living—and swimming— around the caverns and rocks for hundreds of years. Maybe thousands. Though you don't look a day over two hundred," Jack said.

Aquila winked flirtatiously.

Morveren looked sternly at Aquila, then at Jack. She tossed her long red hair over her shoulder. "We know of no escape route that would be useful to you two-legged land dwellersssss," she said distastefully. "All of the wayssss and passages we know are sub-aquatic."

"Well, Torrents and his merry circus of swimming blue horses didn't just take off through solid water, now, did they?" Jack pointed out. "Obviously, one of the caves or tunnels must lead somewhere. 'Cos, last I checked, among the many powers Torrents numbered among his rapidly growing arsenal, breathing underwater wasn't listed."

The crew looked at one another, nodding slowly. Jack did have a point.

"If there is an escape route for those of usssss who breathe the surface air, we are not aware of it," Morveren said, slapping her tail on the surface of the water like an annoyed cat. "It would take you hours to explore the labyrinth of caves that riddle Poseidon's Peak. I believe your first mate said something about there only being fifteen minutessss left before there is no more air left in here."

"He's *my* first mate!" Captain Smith bellowed. "Not Jack's!"

"*I'm* Jack's first mate," Arabella added peevishly.

"Were Jack's first mate," Jack pointed out, "before you and you lot abandoned me completely. But back to the matter at hand. Even with our fifteen minutes—"

"Ten, maybe, now," Mr. Reece interrupted, tapping Jack on the shoulder.

The waterline was up to the crew member's chests.

"Yes, very well. Ten minutes now; thank you, Mr. Reece," Jack said. "We aren't all just going to sit here and wait to drown. There has to be something we can do!"

"Who is sitting?" Jean asked. "I am not sitting anywhere!"

The boy's feet barely touched bottom. His friend Tumen, even shorter, was also placidly trying remain upright. Constance dug her claws deeper into Jean's arms and climbed up his body as the water came dangerously close to touching her tail.

"Jack! Do something!" Arabella cried.

"Oh, excuse me! Perhaps you should address cries of help to your proper captain, mummy dearest Laura Smith," Jack said bitterly, turning to Arabella's mother. "Tell me, *Captain*, what sort of plans do you have prepared for situations such as this?"

"And just how commonplace are situations like this, *Captain* Jack?" Smith shot back.

"Well, if you're me, quite common, actually," Jack replied sincerely.

Jean lifted Constance over his head. Arabella was treading water, trying to keep her head up. The force of the sea coming through the walls grew stronger; cracks became fissures, and fissures became giant gaps. Tumen began to dog-paddle.

"Perhaps we should try plugging the cracks," Mr. Reece suggested. He looked around until he found a piece of stalactite shaped like a thick spear. He wedged it into a fissure. Arabella immediately began grabbing handfuls of looser stones from the small amount of wall around her that was not submerged. She packed these around the stalactite. Tumen held a flat rock against the wall as Jack used the pommel of his sword to try to pound it into place.

For a moment, it looked as though it were going to work.

The water slowed down to a trickle, and everyone sighed in relief. Of course, this was just one crack, and they'd need to repeat it ten, twenty, twenty-five, maybe thirty . . .

"Splendid! Just forty more to go!" Jack said.

"It's no use," Mr. Reece sighed in despair.

"There, there, good try," Jack said, giving him a friendly pat on the back. But it was obvious from the way his eyes moved from left to right, following the cracks, that he was considering despair himself. Jack turned to the mermaids.

"Now, ladies, I wouldn't normally stoop to a level so despicable as to request assistance of you all Scaly Tails. But I fear I have no other recourse . . ." he said.

"How dare you!" Morveren began, directing an angry look at Jack.

"How dare who what?" Jack asked in confusion.

"How *dare* you ask our assistance after not even attempting to assissssssst us in our war with the terrible Torrentsssss?" Aquila explained, equally angry.

"Are you serious?" Jack asked. Then he turned to Arabella. "Are they serious?"

Arabella shook her head, equally confused.

"We're about to drown here!" Jack shouted. "Can we discuss this later?"

"Of all the vile, sssssssslippery, piratical ways in which you have esssscaped your responsibilitiesss, drowning is perhaps the mossst deplorable." Aquala continued. "Especially consssidering the countlessss inappropriate ways you have cheated death and sssslinked away with your mangy hide intact . . ."

". . . And you can't even be bothered to find your way out of thisss chamber," Morveren picked up coldly, "sssso you and your crew can follow Torrents, stop him, and retrieve the Trident . . . sssso we merfolk can once again be free. . . ."

"Oh, Scaly Tails!" Jack shouted, getting angry. "I don't give an albatross's foot about your blasted freedom! And even if I

did—which, as previously stated, I do not—
on my list of things to do, 'Save Scaly Tails'
would fall far, far below 'Remember to brush
teeth.' And I think we all know how infre-
quently I do that. . . ." Jack mumbled the last
part.

"And," he added, just as Morveren was
opening her mouth for a nasty comeback,
"we wouldn't even be down in this dark, wet
deathtrap if you hadn't kidnapped me here!"

He gave Billy Turner a nasty look. The
poor, reluctant pirate had been forced to go
find Jack after the merfolk had captured the
rest of the *Fleur*'s crew.*

"I am truly sorry, Jack," Billy said mournfully. "It truly is my fault. You're right.
You're going to drown because of me."

Jack sighed and rolled his eyes. "Pirates

*See Vol. ii, *Poseidon's Peak* for the full story.

don't apologize, mate. Captain Smith, what type of pirate ship are you running, anyway?"

"Believe me, he's not my first choice for Arabella," Laura said through gritted teeth. "But my first choice, Mr. Reece, feels that if he were to marry my daughter it would be a conflict of interest."

"Oh, Mother, doesn't the fact that I don't love Mr. Reece count fer anything?"

Mr. Reece looked pained by Arabella's admission.

"Oh, Mr. Reece, I'm so sorry, I mean, I *love* ye, I just don't love-ye love ye, y'know? Not like that."

"Er . . . while I'd love to catch up on your love life, Bell, I am more curious to see if anyone else has noticed that the dreaded water is up to our necks now," Jack said, interrupting. It was true. The crew had barely six inches of air to breathe between the surface of the water and the rocky ceiling of the cavern.

"Ummm . . . one last time. Help?" Jack asked the merfolk pathetically.

Morveren dived with snooty grace under the water. Aquila and Aquala quickly followed.

The crew's last hope was gone.

Jack took a deep breath—as deep as he could, considering there was almost no air left in the chamber . . .

. . . and in the next moment, there was none at all. Seawater completely filled the cavern. He and his crew were trapped like figures in a snow globe, floating around, unable to get out.

# CHAPTER THREE

Stupid mermaids, Jack thought, with their stupid songs and their stupid portals and their stupid . . .

Then it hit him.

Portals. The Scaly Tails didn't get into the chamber by any of the tunnels or footpaths. *They came through the pool in the middle of the room!* Which was probably how they left . . . although Jack hadn't exactly seen, as the water was dark and murky. If that was a way in, it was probably also a way out, likely leading to another chamber, or room, or what-have-you. One with *air*. Jack knew this because he had already traveled the whirlpools and water tunnels and portals of the merfolk a few times.*

Of course, he couldn't be sure this one led to someplace with air.

But since his only options were to see where it led or die, he decided on the former. He took one last look at his old crew. Their cheeks were swollen and red as they tried to hold their last gulps of air. Mr. Reece's face was turning bluish.

Arabella stopped thrashing in the water. She had seen Jack start to move away. She desperately reached out to him with one hand. With the other, she was holding Billy's. Billy also didn't struggle, appearing

* In Vols. 2, *The Siren Song,* and 4, *The Sword of Cortés.*

sad and resigned to the fact that it was his fate to die this way.

Looking at Arabella's face, at the pleading and hope he saw there—as well as the slightly waterlogged hue—Jack remembered the last time he and his crew had encountered the mermaids. Arabella had been hypnotized by their song and had jumped overboard, compelled by the music.*

Her face had had the same innocent and trusting affect now.

Jack took her outstretched hand and began swimming down toward the pool, leading her and Billy there. He paused at the marble rim of the pool, pointing into it. He looked back at them to make sure they understood where he was taking them.

Captain Smith and Mr. Reece were close

---

* In Vol. 2, *The Siren Song.*

behind. With them were Tumen and Jean, Constance in his arms.

Jack shook his head to focus. Dizziness almost overwhelmed him as his air continued to run out. Little things were swimming in front of his eyes, and they weren't fish. They were the amorphous, silvery-black blobs that meant he was about to black out.

Using all his remaining strength, Jack kicked down into the pool, dragging Arabella behind him.

A sucking like that caused by a violent whirlpool drew him. He sank down into a giant black vortex. The underwater whirlpool tore him away from Arabella and sent him hurtling through the watery darkness with a force that would have taken his breath away had he had any breath left to be taken. Things rushed by him, gewgaws and trinkets from the treasure room they had just left: wooden teeth, silver candelabra, a pair of women's boots.

Just when he didn't think he could hold his breath any longer, he was violently thrown out of the pool.

He landed on his rump on a very hard, stony surface.

Air! He'd been right. The pool did contain a portal.

Jack slowly stood up, grimacing at the pain of being tossed around. He had surfaced in a small, dimly lit alcove carved into the rock. By the familiar eerie, reddish light that seemed to come from everywhere and nowhere, and the constant dripping sound all around, it was plain that he was still in merfolk territory, probably even still somewhere in Poseidon's Peak, though it was impossible to tell. He could have been in a cave somewhere in far China, for all he knew. The merfolk's portals worked in funny ways.

Just as he turned to see if there were any exits out of the chamber, Arabella and Billy came shooting out of the portal behind him, and slammed right into him.

Jack fell down with a *whump* onto the stony floor. Arabella got up immediately, but Billy sat for a moment, still dazed by his trip.

"Uh, would you mind getting off my back?" Jack demanded. Very calmly, considering.

"Oh, beg pardon," Billy said, nonplussed. Arabella shook her head and held out a hand to get him up.

"All right, then," Jack said, leaping up. "Let's see if there's any—"

*Whump!*

He was knocked down again. Laura Smith and Mr. Reece had come hurtling through the portal and, of course, right into Jack.

"Well done, Jack," Captain Smith said stiffly. "You have saved us all." Despite the obligatory compliment, she was still sneering disgustedly.

"Out of my way!" he yelled, pushing Laura and Mr. Reece aside.

He dived to the side just in time. Jean and Tumen came flying out of the portal, landing right where Jack had been standing. He smirked proudly. "So, now we're all here . . ." he said.

"But, Jack, we're *not* all here. . . ." Jean cried.

Jack knew what was coming.

Suddenly, what looked like an extremely large, particularly wet hairball shot from the portal, whizzed past the crew straight into the opposite wall, and slid down to the cavern floor.

"Constance!" Jean cried.

The mangy cat looked lifeless.

Jean picked her up and she lay limp. Water streamed from her disgusting, matted fur and her mouth hung open, pink tongue lolling to one side. Jack looked at her disgustedly. She was as nasty-looking in death as she had been in life.

Jack motioned quickly for Jean to lay Constance down. Arabella held her hand to her mouth, quivering, while Billy held her tightly. Jean was beside himself, and Tumen rested a hand on his shoulder as he placed the cat on the floor.

Jack poked her in the stomach with the tip of his boot.

She didn't move.

"Yep, definitely dead," Jack pronounced. "Okay, let's go now," he added brightly, turning to leave.

"Jack," Arabella said sternly.

"What?" he asked innocently.

She gave him a look.

The look reminded Jack of the time when she was his first mate, when she would often point out the moral path he should take. He missed those times a little. He missed his crew, too . . . though he'd been denying it to himself since they'd left him. He missed Jean, Tumen. Maybe, just *maybe*, he even missed Constance. A little. A very little. But still, there was a missy-type feeling deep down inside him.

Somewhere.

"Oh, all right," he said, with a roll of his eyes and a big dramatic sigh. He knelt and bent over Constance, rolled up his sleeves, and took a deep breath.

"Right. Make no mistake about this," he said quietly through gritted teeth. "What is about to happen is *not* happening, you never saw this happen, and once it *has* happened— which it won't because it's not going to—*it will have never happened.* Savvy?" He glared at Arabella and the rest of the crew.

They all nodded, half confused, half intrigued. Even Captain Smith agreed to Jack's odd request.

He took another deep breath. He put a pair of fingers over Constance's wet nose and put his own mouth over her disgusting, droolly one. Breathing hard—and trying not to smell anything—he pushed air into her lungs.

Jean clasped his hands together hopefully. A tear formed in the corner of his left eye.

But Constance didn't move.

Water didn't come out of her lungs. She just lay there, cold and yucky, while Jack kept taking breaths and blowing down her throat.

"It's not working," Captain Smith said, with a hint of satisfaction that Jack had failed.

Arabella put a hand on Jean's shoulder.

After all they had been through together, this was how it would end for Constance. On a cold, dark floor in a badly lit cavern.

Jean hugged Arabella and began to sob uncontrollably.

And then Constance threw up. Right into Jack's face.

Half-chewed fish. Bits of grass. The tail of a mouse. A mucus-covered hairball.

Before Jack could react, Constance coughed again—spurting warm, catty seawater into his eyes.

Mr. Reece's face went green at the sight. Billy had to turn away, gagging slightly. Even Captain Smith looked queasy.

Jack calmly walked over to Jean and wiped his face on the Creole boy's shirt. Then he dug the mouse tail and hairball out of his mouth, tossing them to the ground, back into the pile of Constance puke that lay there.

"Constance! You're alive!" Jean shouted. "Oh, *mon ami*, *mon capitan*, We've missed you!" Jean cried, squeezing Jack tightly. Jack carefully and daintily pushed him out of the way, pointing at the vomit stain on Jean's shirt that Jack had left there. He clearly didn't want it back.

Laura Smith—*Captain* Laura Smith— cleared her throat. Just to let them all remember who really was captain around here.

"Ah, *pardon*," Jean said, corrected himself. "Monsieur *former* captain."

Captain Smith smiled, satisfied.

"Thank you for *what*?" Jack asked. "Nothing of any note just happened. And certainly nothing involving a cat."

"*Shhh*," Arabella said, holding up her hand.

Everyone cocked their heads, listening. Half-muffled whispers rose up from below.

Someone, or *something*, was in the chamber with them.

# CHAPTER FOUR

"...*Not our problem*..."

"...*Things we have to do*..."

Arabella and the crew strained to listen. There was some argument going on somewhere in the distance—the cave must have been much larger than they had initially thought. The voices seemed to be coming from below them.

Jack and Captain Smith crept forward slowly trying to find their way. In the darkness, they bonked their heads together as they both leaned forward.

"Ow! You'll rue this day!"

"Shhhhhhhh!" Arabella said, turning around with a finger to her lips.

"*. . . Maybe not such a good plan after all . . .*"

"*Only a* human *would be so callous and untrustworthy. . . .*"

"That's my *foot* yer trodding so lightly on, there," Jack whispered to Captain Smith.

"Ah, I *thought* I stepped in something vile," Laura haughtily shot back.

Arabella closed her eyes in exasperation. She counted to twenty.

When she opened them, her eyes had adjusted to the dark cave. The crew stood at the edge of a slimy, rocky precipice that looked down on a vast chamber a good twenty feet below them.

Jack poked his nose over the side, carefully, because every step on the cave's slippery rocks was treacherous.

The floor below was a maze of beautiful sandy beaches, colorful tide pools, black coral bridges, and thrones. The eerie light of the merfolk's realm made brightly hued fish glow, and seashells sparkle.

"I've been here before," Jack whispered, recognizing the place.

This was the lair of the merfolk, under Isla Sirena.

Last time he had been here, however, the lair hadn't been so empty. The cavern had been filled wall-to-wall with merfolk with tails of all colors. There were the three with blue tails, of course: Morveren, Aquila, and Aquala. They ruled over all of the other ones. The green-tailed merfolk seemed to be some sort of a military unit—well muscled and occasionally armed with spears and tridents. They grouped together in an orderly, rank-and-file fashion. In the back of the hall were the Red-tails, looking generally tired and cowed. They were servants of some sort, forced to do all the jobs none of the others wanted to engage in.

But now it was just the three Blue-tails, beautiful and pale, alone in the vast cavern, sitting on a giant boulder, acting every bit the royalty they were.

"Are you certain we should have left them there to perishhhh, Morveren?"

"We could not risk bringing them here, Aquila. Could not risssk their learning the truth."

Their voices echoed eerily, in musical whispers that were reminiscent of the hypnotic songs they sang.

"But Jack Ssssparrow has been down here before," Aquala said, "and didn't disssscover the treasure trove."

Morveren shook her head.

"We had control over our realm then. We could prevent him from discovering the treasure, if we had to. We could have used force. Now we are alone. Revealing to Jack Sparrow and his crew that there was a passageway back here, back to Isla Sirena, would have been too great a rissssk."

"Risssskier than leaving us three to face him who wields Posssseidon's Trident on our own?" Aquila demanded.

"If that is our fate, sssso be it," Morveren said mournfully. She was, Jack reflected, a bit of a drama queen.

"Since the reemergence of the Purple-tails, our fate has been of utmost concern, has it not? Why complicate it with thissss added threat?" Aquila asked.

*Purple*-tails? Arabella mouthed at Jack.

"I've never seen one," he whispered back, shrugging.

"There has never been a time—at least not within my memory—that any merfolk swam the seas freely. We have lived under a strict code from time immemorial. Those of the purple tail seem to come and go as they please, requiring none of the protection our society affords us. Somehow, they are barely affected by the power of the Trident. If the Trident cannot control them, then neither can we be expected to," Morveren said.

"What problem do they have with the Hierarchy?" Aquala demanded. "It has always been thusss: royal Blue-tails rule, Green-tails fight, and Red-tails ssserve. It has worked just fine for centuries—nay, for *eonssss.*"

"It's just that kind of attitude that made me a pirate," Captain Smith said disgustedly. "Kings and slaves, and all the classes and caste systems in between."

"Aye," Mr. Reece agreed.

"I thought you became a pirate because Da was a drunk and you were sick of your life in Tortuga," Arabella said, a little meanly.

"That, too. And don't question your mother," Captain Smith scolded.

Jack shushed everyone this time. "Hello? Exposition going on here, mates. Enough with the family drama!"

The three Blue-tails below didn't seem to hear the crew's squabbling. While the mermaids' voices carried well from the open, echoey chamber below, Jack's crew's voices were muffled by the rocks they hid behind.

"I've seen them," Morveren continued. "Little groups of Red-tails gathered in the sewage chambers, Green-tails in the barracks. Looking shifty. Whispering. Glancing over their shoulders."

"Sewage chambers?" Jack whispered with a shudder.

"Yes, and sometimes even red and green together!" Aquila piped up.

"And the way they speak . . ." Aquala said thoughtfully, "with all of the whistles and strange clicks of their tongues. It's a code of some sort. It simply musssst be."

"You must see my point, sisters. We needed to nip this little revolution in the bud," Morveren said forcefully. "Who knows what drastic steps they might try next? And what if the Green-tails attempted a coup . . . attacked usssss outright?"

Aquila and Aquala shuddered at the thought.

"And there was that Nautilus we intercepted from that feeble-minded Red-tail," Morveren went on. "There can be no doubt that this . . . *resistance* group is . . . *wassss* . . . planning on sssssstorming Posssssseidon's

Peak and stealing the Trident for themselves."

"Nautilus?" Captain Smith whispered, confused.

"Maybe it's like a missive, or a letter," Arabella reasoned.

"We had to act first—to prevent the disaster that would have been wrought on all of us!" Morveren said, slamming her fist into her other hand. "The Trident was the only possible way to maintain control over these incompetent masssssses!"

"Wait, wait," Jack whispered. "Let me get this straight: the Blue-tails actually used the 'thrice-accursed' Trident of Power to control their own people?"

"They told us *they* got it away from Poseidon so no one could control them anymore. So *they* could be free," Arabella said disgustedly.*

*In Vol. 11, *Poseidon's Peak*.

"Almost makes you feel bad for the merfolk, eh, Jack? I mean, the rest of them. Not these *bleu* ones," Jean said.

"Almost," Jack said. But inside, he was seething. He hated seeing anyone wield such complete power over anyone else. No one should have had that right. Not over him, not over anyone else.

"Was it such a good idea to give the Trident to Captain Torrents, though, I wonder?" Aquala asked thoughtfully.

"Oh, no, they didn't," Jack said, stunned.

"We had no choice," Morveren hissed. "Only a human would be able to keep it out of the hands of other merfolk. We had a deal. He would guard it and share sovereignty over the merfolk with us. The Trident stays out of the resistance's hands, and we keep our status. The only thing we gave up was a little control—and since two-footers have such short lives, it wouldn't have lasted for long. Besides, all they are interested in is treasure. If we kept him buried in a stack of gold he wouldn't have cared *what* went on."

"But like all humans, he was treacherous and lying," Aquala growled, splashing her blue tail in the water. "The moment he had the Trident, he took off with it—bent on controlling all the Seven Seas."

"He didn't even mind that he couldn't use the Trident on us, the Blue-tails," Morveren mused. "He now has an entire army—all of the merfolk—under his control. He commanded them to leave their home here, under Isla Sirena, and pillage and plunder the oceans of the world, giving him all the loot they found. And so, here we are. Alone."

Morveren looked up at the roof of the chamber for dramatic effect. The crew shuffled back quickly from the edge of the precipice in order to avoid being seen.

"We should just be grateful he doesn't know about our own trove. And, above all, the gems," Aquila pointed out.

"We are safe . . . for a time." Aquala added.

# CHAPTER FIVE

"*B*ut what are we as rulers, without merfolk to rule?" Morveren asked.

"Whiny little brats?" Jack suggested in a low voice that the Blue-tails couldn't hear.

"What do we do now?" Tumen whispered.

"I say we leave," Jack suggested.

Everyone stared at him.

"What?" he asked defensively. "Let's just find a way out and go. Forget about the merfolk and their stupid little revolution.

Let's just get out of here and on with our lives. The Scaly Tails are right about one thing: as long as Torrents is reaping in the gold, he's not going to care about Captain Smith or anything else. Plus, he thinks we're dead. And as long as the Blue-tails have to deal with the uprising of the masses, they're not going to care about anything else, either. That's two problems solved right there, as far as I'm concerned."

Jean raised one impish eyebrow. "What about the treasure they mentioned? I mean, don't mistake me, monsieur, I would like to get to that beach and hammock I've been so desiring as soon as possible, but I am surprised the idea of a whole trove of mer-*madam* treasure doesn't tempt you."

"He does have a point, Jack," Arabella said eyeing her old friend speculatively.

"Every time we go after treasure, there is

trouble," Tumen pointed out. "Cursed swords and mystical medallions. Perhaps Captain Sparrow has finally learned his lesson."*

"Why don't we just come back later?" Jack said. "With a ship. And guns. Or nets, really. Get those snotty Blue-tails swept up like cod and cockles . . ." He smiled dreamily at the thought.

"Speaking of ships, what we need to do is find the *Fleur de la Mort*. Immediately," Captain Smith said. "Right now, this crew is useless!"

Everyone glared at her. Billy looked hurt.

"Without a ship. Useless without a ship," she clarified quickly, clearing her throat.

"I feel badly for the . . . Scaly Tails . . . the red ones . . ." Billy began sheepishly. "Seems

*Tumen is referring to the Sword of Cortés and the Sun-and-Stars amulet, the stories of which are told in Vols. 1 through 7.

like an unfair lot for them. Always ordered about by Torrents or the Blue-tails . . . Something should be done about that, don't you think?"

"Fine, you stay and fight their little revolution, Turner," Jack said, throwing up his hands in exasperation. "I'm going to leave. Somehow." He crossed his arms and leaned dramatically against a rock, brow furrowed in thought.

The rock shifted.

Smaller, slimier rocks went bouncing down into the chamber below. They made nasty little plunking noises as they hit the water.

The three Blue-tails looked up, spotting the crew.

Jack gave a weak grin and waved.

"We should have known you wouldn't have been defeated so easily, Jack Sparrow," Morveren cried.

"Defeated?" Captain Smith demanded. "You make it sound like a royal battle! All he had to do was follow you lot out of the chamber!"

"Yes, well, did *you* think of it?" Jack pointed out.

The merfolk immediately closed their eyes and began to sing.

A familiar, dreamy feeling came over Jack and his friends.

Jack remembered the last time the merfolk had tried to hypnotize him. Their song spoke directly to the listener's heart, making him think about the thing he wanted most in the world. More than think, actually. *Concentrate* on. Imagine, to the exclusion of everything else. And then, mad with desire, the victim of the merfolk's song would begin to act very bizarrely.

The last time the merfolk had tried to

entrance Jack, they couldn't do so. The thing Jack wanted most was to be free. So, the Siren Song had no effect on him, as being swayed by it would have meant he was enslaved by it. This time, however, Jack had *another* great wish.

Jack found reality slipping oozily out of his grasp and his vision blurring. A calm sense of almost having what he *wanted*, and the rage of *wanting* it, overwhelmed his senses.

The rest of the crew were also deeply in thrall. Captain Laura Smith was wandering around in circles, pointing and murmuring about the *Fleur*. What she wanted most of all was to get her ship back.

Tumen was fighting with Jean. One boy wanted to return to the Yucatán, the other to travel to the travel to great mystic Tia Dalma, who could lift his sister's curse.

Arabella and Billy shook their fists at the air and spouted semi-intelligible phrases about overcoming the tyranny of the Blue-tails and Captain Torrents.

Constance meowed woefully, smacking her lips. What she wanted to do most of all was chow down on fish.

Jean pulled his sword on Tumen. Laura, sensing that Billy was somehow blocking her way to finding her boat, started beating him about the head with the back of her hand. Billy reeled backward, then gave Laura an unexpected wallop in the stomach. "Tyrant!" he roared.

Soon, all of the crew was fighting amongst itself.

And then someone pushed Constance into the water. She yowled piteously as she hit the water below, a giant, splashing fur ball.

Suddenly she saw the merfolk, right in front of her. Who looked a *lot* like fish—at least from the waist down. Tasty, tasty fish. She began to kitty-paddle toward them, smacking her lips.

Jack wavered on his feet. He wanted . . . he wanted . . .

. . . What was it he wanted?

"Behold! The brave feline has found the source of all tyranny!" Arabella cried, seeing Constance's assault on the merfolk. And with that, she dived in after the cat.

Billy followed her into the water.

"Ow!" Aquala cried, dropping her song. Constance had sunk her teeth into a particularly tender and juicy-looking piece of her tail.

The merfolk's music floundered for a moment, missing a third of its harmony. The friends looking confused, paused in their aimless fighting and swimming.

Jack just wanted to be away from there, he realized, as soon as possible, and never to return to the dank, dark, enclosed world of the nasty Scaly Tails.

But Morveren and Aquila redoubled their efforts. After a moment, Aquala joined them again, twice as loudly as before. She gritted her teeth and held her tail, which was dripping bluish blood into the water. And she also had to keep batting off Constance, who seemed to be in a fish-blood frenzy.

Everyone sank back into their hypnotic stupor.

Captain Laura Smith, falling victim to the dream logic that held that it would perhaps be easier to find a boat *in water*, executed a perfect swan dive into the chamber below.

Mr. Reece dived in right after her, desiring

nothing more than to follow his captain.

Tumen followed and paddled around, looking for a way back to his village in the Yucatán. He bumped into Mr. Reece, who muttered, "Who dares!" and tried to bonk the boy on the head with the pommel of his sword.

Tumen just quietly swam around him, as serene as an otter.

And Jean was sitting on the edge of the precipice, legs swinging in the air, singing sad-sounding songs in French.

"Vile tyrants!" Arabella shouted dreamily. "Oppressors!"

And while she couldn't swim half so well as a mermaid, she managed to get her sword out and lunge at Morveren. The leader of the Blue-tails was trying to concentrate on her song. She had no other weapon but it. But without a sword, she was able to dodge the swimming, hypnotized, and pugnacious Arabella with ease, though she couldn't fight her off completely and sing very well at the same time.

Finally, Jack and his crew began to awaken from their reveries. Jack in particular became clearheaded for just a moment. He looked down at where the Blue-tails were, desperately trying to pick up the threads of the song.

Soon, Morveren was able to find her tune, and the Siren Song again overwhelmed the crew.

But not before Jack's greatest desire had shifted.

Before, it had been to escape from Isla Sirena, in any way possible. But in that split second he had his mind back, he realized something. There was no way he was ever going to escape the island without first defeating those obnoxious Scaly Tails!

And that suddenly became his greatest desire.

With a fierce grin, he jumped down into the water with his knife held between his teeth. Then he swam straight for the merfolk.

Aquila, Aquala, and Morveren nervously watched him come for them. Arabella and Billy were thrashing at the merfolk with their swords—not doing any great damage, but distracting and annoying the three of them. And Constance was diving back and forth, taking little kitty bites out of their tails.

Arabella and Billy pressed their advantage, attacking above the surface, while Jack came at the merfolk from below. The Blue-tails were ill prepared for such an onslaught. For a thousand years their power had been maintained by tradition and use of the Trident. They'd never had to defend themselves physically before—they always had the Green-tails to fend off attackers for them. But now the Green-tails, like the Red-tails, were under the control of someone else—Torrents! And that left the Blue-tails vulnerable.

The three Blue-tails were forced back against the rocky wall of the cavern, singing for their lives.

Then Jack emerged from a crevice in the wall, coming at the merfolk from behind.

"Shut. The. Bloody. Bones. *Up*!" he growled.

Morveren made a sign to her friends, and all three grew silent.

Everyone in the cavern came blinkingly awake. Jean almost fell in the water, not realizing where he was.

"We admit defeat," Morveren said nervously, her hands poised defensively before a dagger Jack had pointed at her throat. "We will allow you to go through one of our portals."

Captain Smith roared in fury and made her way, half slogging, half swimming through the water. She pushed her face into Morveren's and screamed, "You'll do better than that! You will deposit us nearby— or, better yet, *upon*—the deck of the *Fleur*! You . . . *fish sticks*!"

"'Fish sticks?'" Jack asked, looking at Arabella. "That's the best she could do?"

"She's very angry," Arabella pointed out.

Morveren just gave a nasty smile. "All right, then."

The water began to swirl, starting at the crew's feet and moving up to its waists. A current swept the crew out of the cavern through a green and watery tunnel. They were deposited, with a spitting noise, upon the shores of what looked like . . . a completely deserted island.

# CHAPTER SIX

"You have got to be kidding me," Jack said, kicking up a cloud of sand. His words, uttered in a quiet, reedy voice, drifted away on the warm breeze. "Stranded. Again. A—blasted—*gain*. What is this, desert island number two thousand four hundred and sixty-three? Or is it *four*? I've lost count!"

"Oh, stop being so dramatic, Jack," Arabella chastised him gently. It was a beautiful Caribbean day. The lemon yellow sun was drying their wet clothes, and the sand was soft. Landing there didn't feel like the worst fate in the world.

Provided, of course, that there were fresh water, food, a few coconut trees . . . and, eventually, a way back . . .

*"Dramatic?"* Jack snapped. "Dramatic? Just how many times in my life will I be forced to escape a desert island before I can justifiably stomp around being dramatic? On the other hand," he added, partially to himself, rubbing his chin. "I suppose it's good practice, anyhow. If you lot, my loving crew, ever decide to mutiny one day and dump me on a deserted island, at least I'll know how to get off. Magic chariots, mermaid portals . . . maybe riding a turtle or something . . ."

"'You lot'?" Captain Smith said, snorting. *"You* don't have a crew. This crew is mine."

Laura and Jack glared at each other.

Everyone else shifted uncomfortably.

No one had really pledged loyalty to either captain. They had all kept quiet about whether they would rather sail with the imperious, but generally correct Smith or the increasingly scallywaggish (but always fun) Jack.

Arabella cleared her throat nervously. "Uh, mum, only I officially joined your crew. *And* Mr. Reece, of course," she added when her mother's first mate started to object. "We rescued Billy . . . but ye never really gave him a choice in the matter, either."

"Ungrateful lout," Laura growled at Billy.

"But—I didn't—I haven't—" Billy protested. Everyone ignored him.

"Don't start with me, young lady," Captain Smith said, turning back to her daughter. "I'm the only one here capable of leading a decent crew. It's obvious. Just pipe down when adults are making decisions."

"Okay, fine!" Arabella said heatedly, her cheeks flushing with anger. "Ye have two *less* members of 'your crew,' then! Count me out! It's just you and Mr. Reece now. Right, Billy?"

"Um, of course, whatever you say, but really, is this the time—"

"No, it's not the time," Jack interrupted, pointing at the ocean. "*Really* not."

Everyone turned to look.

All along the shore, the perfect, aquamarine water was beginning to boil.

Foaming and churning, the sea began to spit out *things*. Lots of things. Ugly, human-size things. Squirming and writhing in a most unhuman way.

Without a word, everyone drew his or her sword, tensing for battle.

All around them, hundreds—no, thousands—of merfolk came crashing out of the waves. And these weren't the pretty, flowing-haired mermaids of legend. They weren't even the tolerably cute (if annoying) ones the crew had defeated just a few moments before. These were merfolk out of a sailor's worst nightmare.

Most had scaly fish tails. Some had two. Some had three or more, that writhed and squirmed as if they had minds of their own, or they had slimy suckers along their lengths, like an octopus's.

Some had normal legs, ending in webbed feet, or legs that started out normal and then became fused at the feet, becoming one big, ugly flipper.

Some of the merfolk had eels for hair.

Some had, instead of normal mouths, open circles with rows and rows of pointed teeth spiraling back down into their gullets.

Some had horns and fins growing out of their backs.

Some had the soulless black eyes of sharks.

And some even had wings. Slimy ones, like those belonging to flying fish. But instead of just allowing their owners to *glide* over the water, these allowed the dripping nightmares the crew was facing to *fly*.

Those merfolk that could move on land crawled, slithered or humped up the beach toward them, making wet, sucking noises as they went.

"That's a lot of cod to harvest," Jack said, trying to keep it light. But he was calculating the odds—and they weren't good. In fact, they were very, *very* bad.

"But we cannot attack them," Billy protested.

Everyone turned to stare at him.

"Oh?" Jack asked politely. "Because it's seriously looking like they don't have anything against attacking *us*."

The wave of horrible, mutant sea creatures was almost upon them now, roaring and whistling and screaming and bubbling. One lashed out at Jack with a whiplike tentacle. He parried, trying not to look directly at the disgusting mer-creature it was a part of.

"They're only doing it under Torrents's power!" Billy pointed out. "It would be unjust and unfair to do them harm when they are not in control of their own actions! We should spare them their lives."

"It's true!" Arabella agreed fervently.

Captain Smith rolled her eyes. "Oh, all right, then, dear. I'll try my best to try not to hurt them."

And with that, she reached up with her sword and swiped at a flying merman diving at her head. Her rapier cleanly sliced its left wing. The merman crashed to the ground, writhing in agony.

"Mother!" Arabella shouted in horror. Billy put a hand on her shoulder to comfort her, then pulled her close.

"What? I *tried*," Captain Smith responded, shrugging.

Jack tried not to smile. Sometimes he hated Captain Smith . . . and sometimes he absolutely loved her. Though he'd never have let her know that, of course.

Then Jack plunged in to the battle.

It could be truthfully said that no victorious battle had ever been fought like this one. The sheer magnitude and array of merfolk now present had never before been amassed on the surface. Creatures who hadn't felt the light of day on their faces in a hundred years now bared their fangs under unfiltered sun.

Jack fought as he never had before. Squinting and frowning, and occasionally grunting, he pulled every trick, every move he had ever learned or invented. He leaned sideways and kicked at something with the head of a shark while slicing at a merman with scaly white legs. He smashed two mermaids' heads together; they had been attacking from opposite sides. He ducked and rolled between the crablike pincers of a third, while shoving his knife into its bony shell.

Tumen's black obsidian knife sparkled in the sunlight as he spun and ducked and thrust. He murmured fervent prayers in Mayan.

Jean had his friend's back, but their usual jokes were absent. Jean's cheerful smile was gone, replaced by dead earnestness. He dispatched merfolk left and right, with barely a chance to breathe between one and the next.

Captain Smith and Mr. Reece stood side by side, flanking Billy. While Mr. Reece skillfully wielded his cutlass, Laura showed her true pirate stripes: she had her sword in one hand and her knife in the other and was doing equal damage with each.

Billy really did try his best just to defend and not attack. He apologized and used the flat side of his cutlass to try to deliver blows to the creatures' heads. Arabella also tried this.

But no matter what path the crew took, the creatures just kept coming. And while many of them couldn't actually come up onto land or into the sky, many could.

There was no way Jack and his friends could win this battle. Escape was the only option. But how? It was a deserted island, and they had no boat. . . .

Jack thought quickly.

Laura had demanded that the Blue-tails set them on or near the *Fleur de la Mort*. And while the Scaly Tails were annoying and nasty, they usually kept their word.

Jack fought with renewed vigor, working his way over to Captain Smith. During a break in the fighting, when her back was turned, he very quickly picked something out of her pocket.

Captain Smith whirled around, sword raised.

"How *dare* you?" she roared, lunging at him. She was already in a berserk rage because of the battle and advanced on him with a fury he had never seen before. "What did you take? Give it back!"

Jack held up what he had stolen from her: a compass. The one that showed her where the *Fleur* was when its sails were unfurled, making the ship invisible.

"Hello?" Jack shook it. "I mean, you *asked*

to go to your ship. . . . Why didn't you think to actually *look* for it? As—I don't know—a lovely, protected place to escape to?"

She looked at him blankly for a moment. Then her eyes widened in realization.

"I didn't . . ." she faltered.

"*Some* captain," Jack fired at her. "You're all 'my crew' this and 'my crew' that, and you can't even think of the obvious, or go through all your available options. *Strategy*, we call it, mate, strategy."

"Well, I was too busy . . . I was going to look for the *Fleur*, but I got sidetracked," Captain Smith said lamely, making up excuses. "I was too busy saving *your* hide . . . if I hadn't had to do that, I would have found the *Fleur* already."

Jack raised an eyebrow and otherwise ignored Captain Smith. She was obviously reaching for excuses. Jack concentrated on the compass. What he saw made his eyes bulge in amazement.

"What?" Captain Smith demanded, frustrated and embarrassed.

Jack showed her the compass.

The sea was ahead of them. But, according to the arrow, the *Fleur de la Mort* was right . . . *behind* them.

# CHAPTER SEVEN

*W*hen Jack and Laura turned to look, all they saw was dunes and sea grass. Of course, they wouldn't have seen the boat, as it was invisible. But how could the *Fleur* have gotten there? On dry land!

They knew approximately where the boat was—up the beach. It was farther away from the sea and the merfolk who were slowly crawling and slithering out of the sea.

But if the crew could manage to get aboard the *Fleur*, they'd not only be beached, but also *invisible*!

"Everyone!" Jack shouted. "Make your way to the dunes! It's our only chance!"

Captain Smith, who was still red-faced and embarrassed because of not having thought of the compass herself, also piped up. "Ahoy mates," she shouted. "Retreat to the dunes behind us! Immediately!"

"Of all the stupid times . . ." Jack said, rolling his eyes.

"I am still captain here," she reminded him through gritted teeth.

"You'll be a very dead captain in a few minutes if we don't figure out something, fast," Jack pointed out. "Maybe it's your turn to give it a try. The whole 'figuring things out,' like 'using the compass to find a very useful invisible ship' way of figuring things out, I mean."

Captain Smith ignored him. The crew slowly began to move back toward the dunes. The merfolk took this to be a sign of weakness and advanced further.

An extra-high wave crested; horrible, gibbering things snapped at the crew's ankles and reached for their legs. They smelled like watery rot. *Ancient*, watery rot.

Jack was overcome by the stench and had noticed something worse: the tide was coming in. Every wave lapped up higher than the one before it, bringing the army of merfolk closer and closer.

Suddenly, he slammed into something hard.

He reached around with his free hand to rub his aching spine, and his fingers brushed up against something slimy. And wet. And wooden. He turned around, but nothing was there.

It was the *Fleur de la Mort*! Though he couldn't see it, he knew he'd stumbled right into it. Now all they had to do was figure out how to get aboard. The ship itself wouldn't become visible to them until they were on deck. And then they, along with the ship, would become *invisible* to the merfolk.

"Has to be a ladder somewhere," Jack said, trying to feel along the side of the ship with one hand while using his sword to fend off an aerial attack with the other. He was being assailed by a winged mermaid with scales for hair and a tail that came out of the place where her belly button should have been.

There was a sudden crash of thunder. The whole island echoed with it. The brilliant Caribbean midday sun turned black, and white-hot lightning flashed, arcing across the sky in angry jags. The skies turned gray and opened up, pouring rain like a waterfall, with drops the size of rats.

"Oh, no," Captain Smith said, her mouth going slack. She almost threw down her sword in anger and frustration.

Torrents had taken the *Fleur*.

Jack couldn't see him, which meant he was very probably on the deck of the ship, invisible like the rest of it.

Constance yowled in anger and dismay. Her fur was all matted and wet—again. She was probably getting used to being like that, but Jack wasn't getting used to *looking* at her that way.

All at once, Constance leaped out of Jean's arms and went scrambling like a lunatic into the sea grass.

Jean screamed. "Constance! Come back! It's not safe!"

Tumen turned from the fish-thing he was fighting—one that had waddled on shore by walking upright on its hind fins—sighed, and ran after the cat.

And then, suddenly, Constance was

floating in the air, clawing and hissing.

"She has found the ladder!" Tumen realized, cocking his head curiously at the weird sight.

"Tumen, you are a positive master of the massive understatement," Jack replied. He knocked aside a starfish that had been hurled at his head as a weapon and had stuck to his cheek. "Mates! To the cat!"

Captain Smith opened her mouth to give orders over him, again. But Arabella put a hand on her mother's shoulder.

"Just . . . drop it fer now, Mum," she suggested.

The older woman looked miffed, but she sighed, and the mother and daughter ran for the *Fleur*, kicking merfolk out of the way as they went.

The rain was pouring even harder, getting into the humans' eyes and making it harder for them to see. It posed no problem at all for the merfolk. All it did was drive the flying ones closer to the ground, and therefore closer to the people they were attacking.

Tumen was the first up the ladder— behind Constance—and Jack was a close second. He could use only one hand to climb, though. The other still held his sword. The angry, wet merfolk didn't quite understand what was going on, but they saw that their prey was trying to get away.

Arabella and her mom followed, also fighting the harpylike merfolk. Below them were Mr. Reece, Billy, and Jean bringing up the rear.

Behind Jean was a mermaid with a squid for a body from the waist down.

She used four of her tentacles to brace herself on the ground and the other four to grip the bottom of the rope ladder and shake it mightily. She whacked it against the hull of the *Fleur de la Mort*, trying to shake Jack and his friends loose like dirt from a rug. Jack stared down into her horrible gaping maw and sharp, painful-looking beak.

Lightning struck.

The ladder tensed, then violently jerked to one side. Billy screamed as his arm was dragged along the barnacled hull of the ship.

The ladder sagged and swung back and forth, the left side still taut, the right hanging limp. Jack looked up, protecting his eyes from the winged thing attacking him. There was smoke billowing from the top, where the left side *had* been attached to the ship: apparently the lightning strike had severed it. And, judging by the quantity of the smoke, it might not have been the only thing that had caught on fire.

"Blasted pirate! You're setting my ship

aflame!" Captain Smith yelled when she saw the damage to her beloved *Fleur*. She also said many more things, in colorful words that made Billy Turner blush.

Using all her strength, she clambered on up the ladder, ignoring the aerial attacks on her back and legs. She climbed *over* Jack, stepping on his head, and jumped aboard— immediately becoming invisible to him— and anyone else who was not on the ship.

But Jack knew that once he was onboard, everything on deck—the entire ship, in fact—would be visible to him again.

One by one, he and the rest of the crew managed to clamber up what was left of the rope ladder. Each one, setting foot on deck, seemed to disappear to anyone not aboard. This completely confused the merfolk. The flying ones hovered and hissed, darting this way and that. The ones on the ground gibbered and screamed in frustration. Some tried to crawl or swim *through* the ship, which resulted in bumped heads, horns, and fins.

"So what's the scene, mates?" Jack asked jauntily. He gave a friendly little wave to the merfolk, who couldn't see him. Then he turned and faced the rest of his—or Captain Smith's—crew.

It wasn't an entirely comforting scene.

On one side of the ship, Torrents stood at the wheel. His eyes were mad, an almost green-gray that whirled and churned like the sea. A massive storm raged above him, black clouds and lightning boiling out of the air above his head. He held the wheel with one hand and the Trident in the other. He shook it and laughed, throwing his head back like a maniac.

On the other side, toward the stern, stood

Captain Smith, Arabella, Mr. Reece, Billy Turner, Tumen, Jean, and Constance. They looked nervous but ready, steel in their eyes, their hands on their weapons.

They had been living with the specter of Torrents for the past year.

This was it. This was the final showdown.

And not everyone was going to make it out alive.

# CHAPTER EIGHT

With a mighty cry worthy of the greatest captains in seafaring history, Captain Smith drew her sword and lunged at Torrents.

Torrents let go of the wheel. He held his empty hand in the air . . . and a sword materialized in it: a shining, blindingly bright sword made out of pure lightning. It grew out of his fist and arced up until it grew into a claymore.

Captain Smith brought her cutlass down in a beautiful swoop, aiming at Torrents's belly.

He parried with the lightning-sword.

As the two swords clanged together, the electric current traveled up and down the claymore and ran through Laura's sword—and then through Laura.

She spasmed in agony. A horrible crackling noise encompassed her body. A sickly burning smell, of hair and skin, enveloped the deck.

And then she fell down, motionless.

"That was . . . quick. . . ." Jack said, but he couldn't mask the horror in his voice.

"Mother!" Arabella cried.

A true pirate, she didn't run over and embrace her mother's pale, unmoving form the way any other daughter might have. She drew her sword with her right hand and charged Captain Torrents, with a bloody scream.

"I'll kill you!"

Billy followed closely, his own sword drawn.

Arabella swiped at Torrents, ripping a patch of flesh under his arm.

Torrents howled in pain and shot a series of short, deadly lightning bolts at her head.

Arabella ducked, then ran forward, her sword ready. But she knew that any contact with the lightning-sword was deadly and that she would have to avoid it.

She and Billy double-teamed Torrents: Arabella feinted toward his right side while Billy jabbed at his right. Torrents twisted and brought the lightning-sword around, making the pair jump back. He blocked Arabella's next blow with the Trident and scraped the lightning-sword along the deck at Billy's feet. Turner jumped out of the way, and a black, scorched line was burned into the deck, demonstrating the fate he had barely avoided.

But Torrents had other tricks up his sleeve.

He closed his eyes and concentrated. A mighty wind was conjured forth, gusting toward the ship's boom.

Arabella and Billy never saw it coming.

Jean and Tumen cried out, but it was too late. With a sickening crunch, the boom cracked into the backs of their heads, toppling them to the deck.

Jack winced.

Torrents laughed wickedly.

The rain was driving even harder now, no doubt influenced by Torrents's power over the elements. The deck was actually taking on rainwater. It was beginning to rise and slosh over the side. In fact, when he looked overboard, the land was disappearing, too, Jack noticed. Patches of sand and sea grass were fading away as rain fell and the tide came in, flooding the desert island.

The water made it possible for the merfolk to ring the ship on almost all sides now, hooting and screaming and hissing and clawing at it, as if hoping one of the crew would be tossed over the side and into their midst.

Tumen, Jean, Constance, and Mr. Reece took the opportunity to attack Torrents all at once.

They did better than Arabella and Billy and Captain Smith had.

Jean darted in low, swiping at Torrents's feet with his cutlass while Tumen moved in with his obsidian blade. Mr. Reece spun around and tried to attack him from the side. Constance yowled and threw herself at his boot, sinking her teeth into it.

Torrents growled and parried all of the attacks, making sweeping moves with the lightning-sword and the Trident (and shaking

Constance off his foot). The lightning-sword arced brightly into Tumen, who brought his obsidian dagger up to deflect it. Which it did. Jack noticed that the lightning didn't travel up the volcanic glass knife the way it had the metal swords.

Before anyone could recover, Torrents slammed the Trident into the deck. He summoned the power of the winds and caused the rainwater on deck to gather into a giant wave.

Then he sent it crashing into the crew.

The water broke over them, and pulled them across the deck. Tumen, Jean, Mr. Reece, and Constance scrabbled to cling to anything that would keep them from being swept overboard and into the waiting maws of a thousand angry merfolk.

Between the wind and the rain, Jack couldn't see exactly what had happened, but it didn't look as though any of them had made it out of the battle alive. All that was left on deck was Mr. Reece's shoulder belt—*and Tumen's obsidian blade.* The blade was dug into the wood as though Tumen had stuck it there to brace himself against Torrents's wave.

Jack paused, thinking about his crew. Gone. All of them gone. Again.

It was just Jack and Torrents now.

The water around the *Fleur* had risen to such a high level that the ship was now bobbing lightly in the water. Merfolk swam around and around, waiting for whatever came next.

Wind howled around the mad captain's head.

"Give it up, Jack!" Torrents roared with a ghastly grin. "My curse grants me power over the elements, and the Trident affords me power over the seas. It allowed me to take out the tide and beach the *Fleur*. Do you really think you can defeat a man—a *god*—with such powers?"

"I've done it before," Jack pointed out with a smirk. "*Twice*, in fact."

Torrents roared and pointed the Trident toward Jack.

The deck rippled and quaked beneath their feet. It seemed as if it were ready to tear apart at the seams.

"Oh, good move there, mate," Jack said, putting his hands out to steady himself. "Go ahead and destroy the only ship you have—and, as far as I know, the only *invisible* ship on the Seven Seas."

Torrents growled but stopped shaking the Trident.

"And, just a warning," Jack said, drawing his sword and trying to distract Torrents

from his real goal. "*Real* gods tend not to *like* it when you rank yourself among them. Just a warning. You *are* holding Poseidon's Trident, after all."

Torrents howled and lunged at him with the lightning-sword.

Jack dropped his own sword and rolled. He grabbed Tumen's knife out of the hull and jumped back up, just in time to parry an attack from Torrents that otherwise would have taken off his head.

The lightning-sword crashed into Tumen's flashing black obsidian blade. Light scattered, temporarily blinding both of them.

Torrents growled in frustration and waved his hand in the air, whipping up the air with his fiery sword.

A giant gust of wind blew Jack all the way across the deck and into the wooden rails.

Torrents waved his hand again.

Another powerful gust slammed Jack into the side of the cabin, dropping him to the floor like a broken rag doll.

Before he could recover, Torrents wiggled his fingers. Horrible little arrows of wind lashed out at Jack, slicing his clothes and skin with razor-sharp debris picked up from the deck.

He tried to get up, but Torrents slammed the Trident into the deck again. The ship rolled, rocking from side to side.

Jack was bleeding and bruised. Several ribs felt broken, and his left eye was starting to swell.

Torrents approached Jack slowly, relishing his triumph. The cursed captain stood over him, his blazing sword in one hand, the Trident in the other, and a dozen whirlwinds around his feet, ready to kill at his command.

"I'm going to enjoy this," he said with a sick smile. He spread his fingers, and little lightning bolts—not much more than sparks—began to fly at Jack. They scorched his ears, his chest, his knees—and wherever they struck, they burned. But they were only a hint of what was to come. Torrents spread his fingers wider.

Jacked summoned all of his strength and he brought Tumen's blade up, stabbing Torrents in the leg.

It wasn't a fatal blow, but Torrents faltered, unprepared for the attack. He fell to one knee, blood gushing from the wound made by the black knife. The Trident clattered to the deck.

Jack grabbed it.

Torrents lunged at Jack, trying to get it back.

Jack just coolly pointed the Trident at Torrents.

The wood began to buckle and rock under the pirate captain. He stumbled and flailed, trying to get back up. He steadied himself, and Jack pointed the Trident at him. Before Jack could even think about using the Trident against Torrents, the staff filled up with a bizarre energy Jack hadn't felt since he'd last held the Sword of Cortés. The energy blast from the Trident propelled Torrents right over the side of the *Fleur*.

Jack glanced over the edge as Torrents plunged into the waiting arms, tentacles, and fins of a thousand angry merfolk who were no longer under his control.

There was a moment's stillness, with Torrents floundering in the waves, and then the merfolk spotted him. They began to swarm around him.

Jack turned away. It was obvious what was going to happen next, and it wasn't going to be pretty. The merfolk were on Torrents like seagulls on a whale carcass, and that was something too terrible for even Jack Sparrow to witness.

Almost immediately, the sky began to brighten. The clouds disappeared, and the rain stopped. The sun came out. The ocean calmed.

Jack looked back out at the water. The merfolk were still there . . . but Torrents was nowhere to be seen. Jack shivered.

He turned around.

The deck of the *Fleur* made for a much happier picture: the crew had survived—though barely—and were slowly rising and regrouping on deck. Jean and Tumen were clambering back on board, having managed to hang on to the sides for dear life. Mr. Reece and Constance untangled themselves from the nets and the barrels where they had been trapped. Arabella was tsk-tsking over the bump on the back of Billy Turner's head, and Captain Smith was groaning, rubbing her aching, burned back.

"Good morning, mates," Jack said brightly. He walked jauntily over to the wheel of the ship and gave it a possessive pat. He grinned at Laura. "Look what *I've* found, while you were cat napping."

He lifted the Trident.

Captain Smith just groaned some more, collapsing glumly back on to the deck.

"Blasted Pirate Code," she grumbled.

"Yep, no Pirate Code applies to me. Not a pirate here," Jack said proudly.

"No, you're not. . . . Not yet anyway," Laura said, grinning mysteriously.

# CHAPTER NINE

Jack wandered over to the side of the ship and peered over.

The merfolk treaded water, silent.

Jack sneered. What now?

Even in their quiet state, Jack found them repulsive. Large, expectant eyes were lidless and often covered in sea snot. Mouths, hanging open in anticipation, foamed, and forked tongues flicked out, testing the sea air. There were even one or two babies, held protectively in the arms of their parents.

"Ugh," Jack muttered to himself.

A knowing look and mischievous grin came over Captain Smith's face. It was clear she had an idea. "Mr. Reece, furl the sails," she commanded, and Mr. Reece obeyed, making the ship—and everyone on it—visible once more.

Everyone—including Jack.

He gave the Trident a tentative wave.

The crowds of merfolk cheered, hissed, clapped, and gibbered.

Jack forced a grin.

Laura grinned, too, satisfied that she'd made Jack uncomfortable.

The merfolk with wings were landing on the deck, as gracefully and quietly as they could. Some of the landings were squishier and wetter than others. And stinkier.

"Ugh," Jack said again, upset at what the creatures were dripping onto the deck. Even the usually diplomatic Arabella was doing her best not to make a face.

"Seriously now," Jack whispered to her, "what about those mermaids of legend? With the pretty"—he brushed at his hair—"and the porcelain"—he indicated his face—"and, the most important bit—" He moved his hands through the air to indicate a feminine body.

"Jack!" Bell snapped. "Maybe they think *you're* ugly."

"At least *I* don't stink," Jack shot back. But then he raised his arm and gave his armpit a tentative sniff. "Much."

He sighed and cleared his throat, assuming what he thought was a royal stance.

"All right then, my—uh—gibbering and loyal subjects. This here Trident thing means I'm your king now. And my first royal proclamation is that you are all free to go. And by 'go' I mean, really, *go*. Somewhere very far from here. Far from this ship. Far from me, in particular. Savvy?"

He gave a friendly little royal wave, cupping his hand, and turned to go.

"I am afraid that is not possible, sire," a voice called out from the sea.

Jack sighed, closing his eyes and dropping his shoulders. He should have guessed it wouldn't have been that easy. Although being called "sire" wasn't half bad. He didn't hate the sound of it at all.

He stomped regally back over to the rail and leaned over. "Who said that?" he shouted, waving the Trident for effect.

A merman leapt out of the water to get his attention.

"I did, sire."

This member of the merfolk was much more traditional-looking than the others: a handsome, human-male upper body and a fish's lower body. *Purple.* In fact, he looked a lot like the Blue-tails except for the shade of his scales. "I am called Tonra, my lord."

"Now, *he* looks like I always imagined a merman to look," Captain Smith said thoughtfully, with a flirtatious smirk.

"For once, you and I are in agreement, Mum," Arabella said, sighing dreamily.

"Now, what exactly do you mean, 'impossible'?" Jack said, turning the conversation back to Tonra and the matter at hand. "I've got the Trident here, mate. I talk, you walk. Or swim. Or leap. Or whatever it is you folks do."

"My lord, my people thank you for your kindness and generosity . . . but I beg your leave to show you why we are not 'free to go.' Why we will *never* be free."

Tonra motioned to the water beside him.

"You want *me* to go down *there*?" Jack asked, incredulously sneering to the point of hilarity. There was no way he was diving down of his own free will into the crowd of monsters swirling below.

"Oh, go on, your people want you," Captain Smith said with a snicker. And then she kicked Jack in his royal rear right off the deck.

"Mother!" Arabella shouted.

Falling through the air, Jack frowned, never loosening his grip on the Trident. The merfolk quickly cleared a place for him to land. He hit the water with an amazing splat, in a belly flop that sent great sheets of water in all directions.

Jack surfaced and growled up at the ship, seawater dripping into his eyes. Captain Smith gave him a friendly royal wave of her own. Jack had landed right next to Tonra, whose incredibly handsome, fresh face was grating on Jack's nerves.

A whirlpool formed quietly next to them, disappearing into the sea below.

"My lord, will you follow me?" Tonra entreated, as eager as a boy who wanted to play catch with an older brother.

"I suppose I must," Jack said wearily. "The burdens of running a kingdom are almost too much for my royal self to bear. . . ." And then they dived down.

Now long used to the portals of the mermaids, Jack crossed his ankles, relaxed, and enjoyed the ride. Tonra looked back at his guest anxiously, but Jack just yawned out a stream of air bubbles as if he did this every day. Which, recently, seemed to be the case.

The portal spat him out just a minute later. Prepared for it this time, Jack landed gracefully on his feet in a move that would have made any gymnast proud. They were back in the giant reception chamber, the one where they had fought the Blue-tails just a few hours before.

Aquila, Aquala, and Morveren were still there.

When they saw Tonra, they hissed and gibbered as disgustingly as any of the grosser, squiddy merfolk would have done.

"You! You dare to come back here!" Morveren screeched.

"Yes, I dare," Jack said, striding forward through the water. Then he realized they weren't talking to him. They were talking to the merman next to him. "Oh, er, *us* dare come back here. Yes. You all know each other?"

"He isss the leader of those who dare foment revolution!" Aquila said, hissing with anger.

"I'm liking you more and more, Tuna," Jack said cheerily to Tonra. The merman beamed back. "And it's not just your handsome mug."

"Merfolk have lived happily for a thousand years under the guiding hand of the Blue-tails," Morveren said, regaining control of her voice. "Why do you need to change that?"

"'Lived,' perhaps," Tonra said with feeling. "But not happily. We have been serving and slaving for the privileged few for far too long. . . . Doing your dirty work while you do nothing at all!"

"We rule; that is our lot," Aquala said snootily.

"While you sit up here, and . . . and . . . *comb your hair*," Tonra sputtered with righteous indignation, "who tends the kelp beds? Who harvests the sea slime? Who herds the algae?"

"Does algae really *need* to be herded?" Jack asked, feeling slightly sick.

"Everyone else, everyone but you," Tonra said. "And the Red-tails do all your dirty work, and capture your prisoners, and salvage your loot. . . ."

"Loot?" Jack asked, eyes widening with interest.

"It is a system that has worked well for a thousand years!" Morveren said to Tonra.

"Only because of the Trident and the harsh hands wielding it!" Tonra shot back.

"Yes, and thank you, Jack Sparrow, for returning to us what is rightfully ours," Morveren said with an unctuous smile. She put her hand out.

"Well, technically, it's rightfully *mine*, because I won it fair and square," Jack pointed out. "In a battle *you lot* thrust me into in the first place."

131

Morveren gave another hiss, and she and her fellow Blue-tails swam forward, ready to attack.

"Up-bup-bup!" Jack said, shaking his finger at them with one hand and shaking the Trident at them with the other. The earth began to quake under the water. Rocks fell from the ceiling above. Terrified, the Blue-tails backed off, huddling against each other.

"And try any of your Siren Song stuff and the whole ceiling comes down. Savvy?" Jack said. Then he turned to Tonra and asked "Was this what you needed to show me, Tuna?"

"Tonra, my lord," the merman said shyly.

"'Cos I've seen this lot before, and I agree with you completely already. You had me at the words *Yes, I dare . . .*"

"Thank you for that . . . support, my lord,"

Tonra said, "but this is not all I wanted to show you. There is further evidence of their tyranny."

The merman swam around the three mermaids, shooting them a nasty look. Jack followed as best as he could, hip-deep in water.

"You will pay!" Morveren promised, acid in her voice. "Traitor! No two-footer has ever treaded into such sacred territory as the trove! You will *pay!*"

At the back of the chamber was a locked door, set in a small alcove. Tonra gestured politely to Jack.

"No problem, mate!" Jack said cheerfully. He gently tapped the Trident on the door, and the lock shattered easily and silently. "Handy thing, this," he mused, opening the door and following the merman in.

What he saw inside made his jaw drop.

The walls and ceiling were lined with hundreds of little recesses, like those carved into walls for candles. But instead of candles there were gems: huge glowing and twinkling gems, in all colors of the rainbow. Red, green, yellow, orange, chartreuse, aquamarine, teal, brown, black, tan . . . They flickered and cast multicolored shadows on the wall.

"It's making me a little sick, actually," Jack admitted.

"Each of these stones represents . . . *is* . . . one of the different types of merfolk. One was created for each kind of mer. The Trident affects these gems, thus indirectly controling the merfolk. Poseidon himself had them created by the clever god Hephaestus, and gathered them here deep within Isla Sirena. Look." He pointed to a locked metal cabinet hanging on the wall. A faint blue light shone through an intricate, rusted keyhole. "Over a thousand years ago Morveren's ancestors had the blue stone—the one which controls the Blue-tails—locked in a separate chamber designed by another diety—the goddess Calypso. The chamber is shielded from the Trident—and thus the Trident has no power over them. The Blue-tails have used that to their advantage. They kept control of the Trident and therefore the rest of us, and we have been enslaved to them ever since. When your foe, Torrents, usurped the Trident, he had control over all us merfolk—every breed and variety, as you saw. Every one of our kind except those of the Blue tail."

Tonra then turned and pointed to a dimly flickering purple stone. It had a jagged gash through it, as if it had been formed improperly.

"Cut, clarity, carat, and color, my friend;

that is not a valuable diamond," Jack observed.

"That is the stone of my people, the Purple-tails," Tonra said. "It is flawed, as you see, and therefore it does not hold absolute power over us, only influence."

He sighed deeply, gesturing sadly at the stones. "So as I said, sire, we will never truly be free. Not as long as these stones exist. Not as long as the Trident has any power over us."

The word *free* reverberated in Jack's soul. Freedom was what he himself had been searching for over the last year. Freedom over his fate, over his future, over his destiny . . . All he wanted was to sail the seas freely, going where he wanted when he wanted, with whomever he wanted. To be free from imperious parents and ancient curses and anyone else trying to tell him what to do. How could he truly be free with the weight of an entire race of beings on his back? It wasn't just that this power, this responsibility, was far too great for Jack Sparrow. He just really didn't care enough about managing other people's lives. He had enough trouble managing his own.

"Well . . . Tuna . . ." Jack said slowly and seriously, looking at all the pretty, glittering gems. "This may not make any sense to you—I'm not sure it makes any sense to me—but the only way for me to be free is for you to be free. So, in my first official act as ruler of the merfolk, I'd like to ask you to step outside for a moment."

Tonra looked confused but hopeful.

"As you wish, sire," he said, gracefully gliding out under the water and closing the door behind him.

A great rumbling came from the room. Tonra and the Blue-tails looked at one another nervously. Around the edges of the door, light flashed in a thousand different colors. There was a huge explosion, and rumbles and crashes like a thousand panes of glass breaking.

Then there was silence.

The door opened, and Jack came out, multicolored smoke rising around him. Behind him, every crystal in the room had been destroyed. A rainbow of fine, sparkling dust floated up in the room. The metal chamber that Calypso had created for the Blue-tails was torn off the wall and lay on the floor.

"Fool! You have no idea what you have done, or the destruction you have wrought!" Morveren cried.

Jack waved his hand at her dismissively, then laid it on Tonra's shoulder.

"You're all free now," Jack said.

"Sire, if you don't mind my interference, I

believe we will need a steady hand to guide us. We have been captive for so long, we could fall into ruin gaining our freedom so quickly. Will you be that guiding force?"

Jack wrinkled his nose and sneered. He had never thought of himself as a steady hand, or proper guide, before.

"Sure, yes, of course," Jack said flippantly. "But I can't be down here overseeing things all the time. I'm going to need a first mate down here. . . ." Jack winked at Tonra.

Tonra glowed with pride. The Blue-tails grew livid.

"You listen to him now, savvy?" Jack said, shaking his finger at the three Blue-tails. As if they were younger sisters who needed to mind. "Now, how in Hades do I get out of here? I can't take the smell anymore. Ever again, really."

"My lord—"

"*Jack*," Jack said, correcting him, with a gentle smile. "*Captain* Jack. Sparrow."

"Captain," Tonra said with a grin, "I bid you good-bye, with the heartiest thanks of the merfolk."

Tonra lifted his hands, a watery portal opened in the waves, and Jack jumped through, catching a glimpse of the three Blue-tails as he shot from the room. He couldn't be sure, but he could have sworn that Morveren had collapsed on the chamber floor.

# CHAPTER TEN

*J*ack popped up out of the water right next to the *Fleur de la Mort*. The merfolk were gone—and so was their stink.

Billy dropped a rope ladder—a new, whole one—over the side of the *Fleur*. Jack grabbed it with his free hand and scrabbled up, agile and light-footed. He threw himself over the rail and onto the deck with a dramatic leap.

The entire crew greeted him, and Arabella nudged her mother impatiently.

"Do ye not have something to say, Mum?" she prodded.

Captain Smith sighed. Then she cleared her throat and strode forward, approaching Jack. He leaned back on his heels and waited with amusement.

"Thank you, er, for saving my life," Captain Smith said, very reluctantly.

"Why, it was no problem at all, Laura—" Jack began.

". . . But don't ever expect me to repay the favor!" she finished, glaring at him. Then she turned to her daughter. "How was that, dear?"

Arabella shrugged, sighing. It was obviously the best her mother could manage.

"And to *show her thanks*," Arabella said, "Mum has asked that you *join* us aboard the *Fleur*."

Captain Smith looked so pained, so tight-jawed, that Jack was pretty sure she was going to throw up right then and there. He smirked. She wanted him aboard her ship about as much as she wanted a boil on the tip of her nose.

In short, Jack saw that he could have a lot of fun on the captain's ship.

"Of course, by the Code, Captain, the *Fleur* is rightfully mine, anyway," he said nonchalantly. He put his hands behind his back and strolled down the deck. "I did save her, after all," he mumbled as he walked away.

Laura almost exploded in rage.

Then she took a deep breath and began doing captainy things: ordering people and strutting about. That always made her feel better.

"Billy, batten down those barrels over there! Jean and Arabella, unfurl the sails; make us invisible! I want us out of here—

*away from here*—as quickly as possible! Mr. Reece, to me! Tumen! Plot us a course for someplace interesting!"

Jack stood out over the bow, tuning out the commotion behind him. Above, a large, warm, orange sun sank down slowly into the dusk. Below, the azure seas of the Caribbean lay placidly in every direction, sparkling where a small wave broke or a fish jumped out of the water. Ahead, the water stretched all the way to the horizon—all the way to forever.

Jack had done many exciting things in the course of his adventures thus far. But nothing as big—nothing as *important*— as freeing an entire race of beings. The merfolk were free now, and they would soon be building a better life for themselves. All because of him.

Of course, he had also just become their

ruler—but really, was that such a bad thing?

"King of the merfolk," he mused to himself.

He wondered if life would always be this good.

Constance, for once dry and fluffy—though still kind of gross and mangy—gave a little meow and rubbed against Jack's leg.

Jack picked her up and gave her a chin a scratch, then rubbed her head. She purred and pushed further into his arms.

He reached into his pocket and pulled out a gem. A glittering stone that glowed blue in the sunlight—the same color blue as Morveren's tail.

Who knew when it would come in handy? The quest for freedom was often fraught with peril and danger, battle and trickery. He put the stone back in his pocket and patted it lightly.

Then he smiled and looked out on a glorious sunset and a future full of possibility—it was the boldest horizon he had ever seen.

*The End*

Though this is the final book
in the epic story of Jack's first year at sea,
there are more Jack Sparrow and
Pirates of the Caribbean stories sailing your way
faster than you can say "savvy."
Read on to see what's in store, mate!

*Available January 2009*

# JACK SPARROW

## The Tale of Billy Turner (and other stories)

Wonder what Jack's crew did aboard the *Fleur de la Mort* after leaving Jack and the *Barnacle* in New Orleans at the end of *City of Gold*? Want to know how they met Billy Turner? This double-sized volume will tell that tale along with other rare or previously unpublished stories about young Jack and his crew. The book also includes an exclusive story that ties into the swashbuckling new series Legends of the Brethren Court.

*And beginning Fall 2008 . . .*

Disney

# PIRATES of the CARIBBEAN

# LEGENDS OF THE BRETHREN COURT

### *The Caribbean*

Rob Kidd

Based on the earlier adventures of characters created
for the theatrical motion picture,
"Pirates of the Caribbean: The Curse of the Black Pearl"
Screen Story by Ted Elliott & Terry Rossio and
Stuart Beattie and Jay Wolpert,
Screenplay by Ted Elliott & Terry Rossio,
And characters created for the theatrical motion pictures
"Pirates of the Caribbean: Dead Man's Chest" and
"Pirates of the Caribbean: At World's End"
written by Ted Elliott & Terry Rossio

# CHAPTER ONE

"**J**ack!"

The sun shone merrily on the sparkling blue sea, and on the crisp black sails and gleaming scrubbed decks of the *Black Pearl*. Up at the prow of the ship, a dashing pirate stood proudly, arms akimbo and legs braced against the rolling waves, his dark hair flying in the wind. He turned his head slightly and grinned, letting the sunlight sparkle grandly off his gold tooth.

"JACK!" the voice behind him said again, exasperated.

Jack Sparrow still did not respond. He tried a different way of tilting his head, setting his hat at a jaunty new angle.

The barrel of a pistol poked him forcefully in the ribs.

"I don't know what you're playing at," his first mate snarled from the other end of the pistol, "but I *know* you can hear me, Jack."

"Oh, sorry," Jack said, spinning around with a little wave of his hand. "I presumed you must be addressing some *other* Jack, one who was not captain of the finest ship to ever sail the Seven Seas—since *surely* if you were addressing *me*, you would have said 'Captain Jack,' isn't that right?"

His first mate heaved a deep, irritated sigh, his scraggly red beard quivering. "My apologies, *Captain* Jack."

"That's much better," Jack said, tapping him lightly on the head. "When we get our new crew in Tortuga, they'll be looking to you for how to behave, savvy?" He sauntered back toward center deck, then turned, squinting, as a thought struck him. "Oh, and really? Ostrich feathers, Barbossa? Don't you think that's a little much?"

Barbossa narrowed his eyes as Captain Jack Sparrow sallied off along the deck. He self-consciously touched his new hat, resplendent with enormous ostrich feathers. "We're a-coming up on Tortuga now, *sir*," he called.

"Excellent," Jack called back. "Let's see if we can find some *real* pirates there."

The few remaining crewmembers glared at him.

"I mean, in addition to you fine . . . swarthy . . . er, burly ruffians," Jack added.

It was surprising how fickle pirates could be. One tiny misadventure—one mislabeled treasure map, one chest of mold instead of gold—and they scattered to the winds, grumbling and muttering and throwing dark glances back at their captain. As if it were his fault! So what if he was the one who'd bought the map? Any other pirate captain would have done the same at that ridiculously low price.

Well, no matter. If there was one thing that was easy to find in the Caribbean, it was a fresh supply of pirates. With his loyal first mate, Barbossa, at his side, Jack would sweep into Tortuga and no doubt the best pirates would fall all over themselves to join him.

They only had to take one look at his magnificent ship to see the advantages of being part of Jack's crew. The *Black Pearl*! Fastest ship in the Caribbean! This was a far cry from his first command, the lowly *Barnacle*. Pirates dreamed all their lives of having a ship like the *Pearl*, and now it was his: risen from the depths of Davy

Jones's Locker like the Kraken from the deep.

And all he had to do to get it was barter away his soul. Jack straightened his hat, brushing away the uneasiness that came with that thought. He didn't have to worry about his bargain for another thirteen years. He'd find a way to deal with it by then. For now, he had thirteen years of freedom to look forward to—thirteen years of freedom with his loyal crew and his splendid ship.

First he just had to find that loyal crew.

\* \* \* \* \* \*

In this first volume, Jack assembles a new crew that includes his first mate, Hector Barbossa, the brooding Billy Turner, and a certain sailor named Jean that Jack's known since they were both kids. Also on board is a host of new and daring cohorts in Jack's quest for absolute freedom—the royal pirate Carolina and her partner-in-crime Diego; the truly fearsome (you'll need to read it to see why) Catastrophe Shane; Jean's cousin, Marcella; and Tia Dalma's mysterious servant, Alex. But it doesn't take the crew long to find trouble—in the form of Villanueva, the Pirate Lord of the Adriatic Sea.

This series, in six volumes, will see Jack and his new crew sail the Seven Seas and encounter the Pirate Lords that control them. Get ready for a trip around the world, traveling the only way to go—aboard the legendary *Black Pearl!*